First U.S. Edition

First published in Great Britain by Heinemann, London

ISBN 0-316-15189-0

Library of Congress Catalog Card Number 90-53552

Library of Congress Cataloging-in-Publication information is available.

10 9 8 7 6 5 4 3 2 1

Printed in the Netherlands

Hurray for Ethelyn

Babette Cole

Little, Brown and Company   Boston Toronto London

Ethelyn was a smart rat. She wanted to be a brain surgeon when she grew up.

She was so brainy that she won a scholarship to go
to Cheddar Gables College
for Richer Ratlettes.

"It looks a bit fancy, Ethelyn," said her brother, Errol.

Miss Nibble, the principal, looked nice enough . . .
but some of the other ratlettes
looked awful!

There was a mean gang of school bullies
led by Tina Toerat!

They were jealous because Ethelyn was so smart!

They put ink in Ethelyn's underwear!

They pulled her whiskers,

called her bad names,

and wouldn't play with her.

"You'll soon settle in," said Miss Nibble, "and you'll feel better after a good night's rest."

But the dormousery was haunted!

So when Miss Nibble's expensive French cheeses
disappeared, everyone blamed the ghost . . .

... until the cheeses were found under Ethelyn's bed!

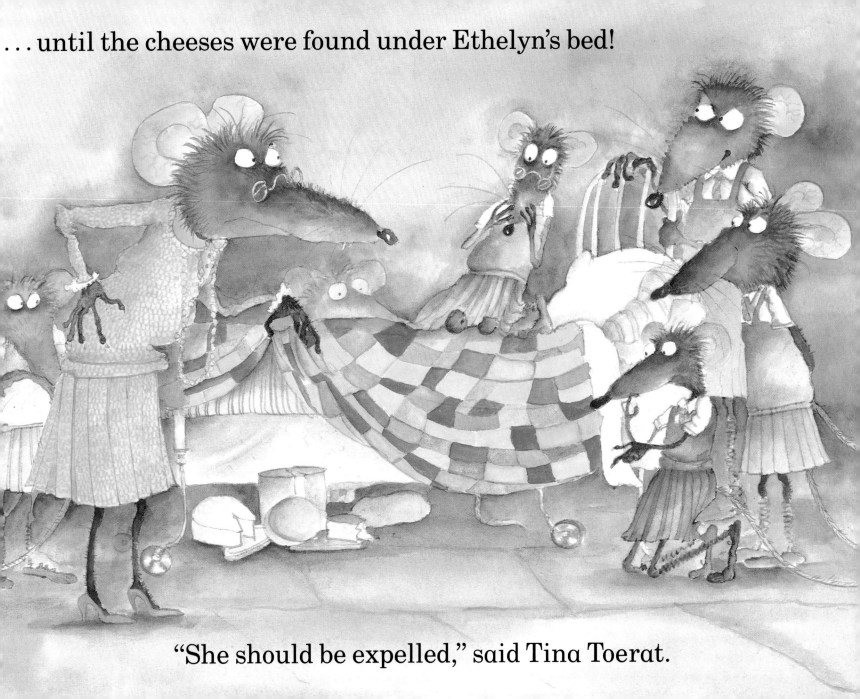

"She should be expelled," said Tina Toerat.

"It wasn't me!" said Ethelyn.

But they locked her in the attic anyway,
until they could decide what to do with her.

Ethelyn wrote to her brother.

Dear Errol,
    Please come and
rescue me. I am so
miserable,
        love Ethelyn.

Eventually
she heard a
scratching noise.
It was Errol!

During their escape they saw the ghost!

"There's your thief," said Errol.

"It's Tina Toerat's gang," squeaked Ethelyn.

The gang split . . .

. . . but Tina got stuck!

"No time for the ambulance," said Ethelyn.

"Her brain's probably scrambled."

Ethelyn operated
immediately.

Of course it was a complete success.

"You're the cheese knees, Ethelyn," said Tina.
"I'm sorry I was such a rat!"

So Ethelyn became the most popular student in the school and the most brilliant brain surgeon ever.

Hurray for Ethelyn!